DATE DUE

Demco

EXPLORING OUR
UNIVERSE

ASTEROIDS, COMETS, AND METEOROIDS

LAUREN KUKLA

Checkerboard
Library

An Imprint of Abdo Publishing
abdopublishing.com

abdopublishing.com

Published by Abdo Publishing, a division of ABDO, PO Box 398166, Minneapolis, Minnesota 55439. Copyright ©2017 by Abdo Consulting Group, Inc. International copyrights reserved in all countries. No part of this book may be reproduced in any form without written permission from the publisher. Checkerboard Library™ is a trademark and logo of Abdo Publishing.
Printed in the United States of America, North Mankato, Minnesota
102016
012017

Design: Emily O'Malley, Mighty Media, Inc.
Production: Mighty Media, Inc.
Editor: Paige Polinsky
Cover Photograph: NASA
Interior Photographs: AP Images, p. 15; Getty Images, p. 17; Mighty Media, Inc. p. 9; NASA, pp. 7, 13, 19 (bottom), 21, 25, 27, 28; Shutterstock pp. 5, 10, 23; Wikimedia Commons, p. 19 (top)

Publisher's Cataloging-in-Publication Data

Names: Kukla, Lauren, author.
Title: Asteroids, comets, and meteoroids / by Lauren Kukla.
Description: Minneapolis, MN : Abdo Publishing, 2017. | Series: Exploring our universe | Includes bibliographical references and index.
Identifiers: LCCN 2016944822 | ISBN 9781680784039 (lib. bdg.) | ISBN 9781680797565 (ebook)
Subjects: LCSH: Asteroids--Juvenile literature. | Comets--Juvenile literature. | Meteoroids--Juvenile literature.
Classification: DDC 523.44--dc23
LC record available at http://lccn.loc.gov/2016944822

CONTENTS

MISSION
METEORS AND MORE

Have you ever seen a meteor streak across the sky? Its brief burst of light can be exciting and beautiful. Maybe you have even witnessed a meteor shower.

Comet Dust

Meteor showers are caused when Earth passes through comet debris. Comets are big, dirty snowballs that orbit the sun. As a comet gets closer to the sun, it heats up. The sun's heat causes the ice to disintegrate. This releases a trail of rock and dust into space. When Earth passes through this trail, we experience a meteor shower.

Meteor, Meteoroid, or Meteorite?

Asteroids are rocky bodies that orbit the sun. When asteroids enter Earth's atmosphere, they burn up in a

The Perseid meteor shower occurs every August. It's possible to see up to 100 meteors an hour during the shower!

bright flash. This flash is called a meteor. If a large asteroid hits Earth, it can cause great destruction. But small asteroids rarely cause damage. These are called meteoroids. Sometimes small pieces of meteoroids land on Earth's surface. These are meteorites.

CHAPTER 1

HURTLING THROUGH SPACE

Our solar system contains billions of asteroids, comets, and meteoroids. Many were created around the same time as the solar system. They act like snapshots of its past.

To watch a comet form, you would need to travel back 4.6 billion years. Then, the solar system was a cloud of dust and gas particles. Over millions of years, gravity combined these particles. They formed a star. This star became our sun.

Swirls of dust and gas orbited the young sun. Eventually, the orbiting gas and dust particles **collided** and combined. They formed lumps that grew larger.

DID YOU KNOW ?

The young solar system was a violent place. Asteroids and comets frequently struck the planets. The moon's many craters are proof of our solar system's rough past.

The Comet NEAT streaked across the sky on May 7, 2004.

The biggest lumps became the **cores** of the solar system's eight planets. Smaller lumps in the outer solar system were far from the sun's heat. They became icy comets. Lumps nearer to the sun became rocky asteroids.

CHAPTER 2

COMETS

Most comets exist in our outer solar system. But sometimes a comet gets knocked into a new orbit. It travels closer to the sun. This new path may bring the comet nearer to Earth, sometimes close enough to be seen.

The comets seen from Earth usually come from the Kuiper belt. The Kuiper belt is a disk of frozen celestial bodies. It is very far from the sun. Most Kuiper belt comets have **orbital periods** of less than 200 years. They are known as short-period comets.

Other comets orbit the sun for thousands of years. These are known as long-period comets. Such comets orbit the sun from the outer edges of our solar system. This region is known as the Oort Cloud. The gravity of nearby stars can affect these comets' orbits. When this happens, Oort Cloud comets can be hurled toward the sun.

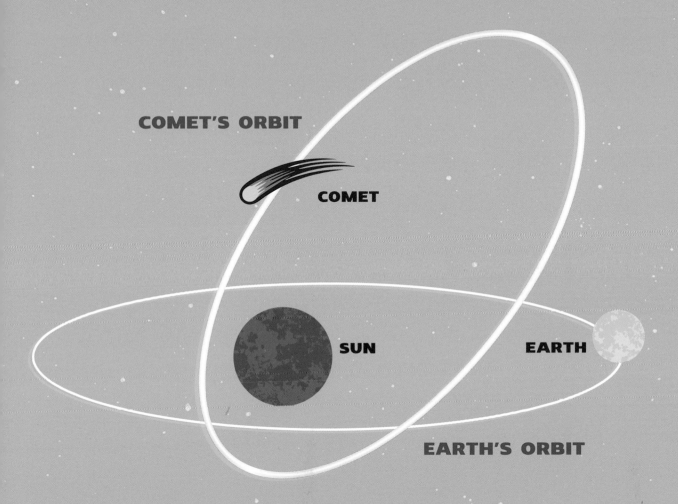

COMET'S ORBIT

COMET

SUN

EARTH

EARTH'S ORBIT

Encke's Comet has the shortest recorded orbital period at 3.3 years. Comet West has the longest at 250,000 years.

Comet NEAT was discovered in 2002.
Its orbital period is about 37,000 years.

A comet begins its journey as a chunk of frozen gas and dust. This chunk is called a nucleus. It is usually less than six miles (10 km) across. As the nucleus approaches the sun, it heats up. The ice boils away. This creates a cloud of gas around the comet, known as the coma.

The coma grows as the comet gets closer to the sun. It can spread out as far as 50,000 miles (80,000 km). The comet also develops a long tail. This tail always points away from the sun. It can stretch for up to 600,000 miles (970,000 km).

The comet eventually returns to the edge of the solar system. Its coma and tail shrink as it leaves the sun behind. The comet returns to being an icy nucleus. But it leaves a trail of dust and ice, which becomes a meteor shower!

DID YOU KNOW ?

Comets contain many of the elements necessary for life on Earth. Many scientists believe comets may have delivered these elements to Earth when the planet was very young.

CHAPTER 3

ASTEROIDS

Asteroids are found much closer to Earth than comets. Asteroids are rocky bodies too small to be considered planets. Most have a lumpy shape. Asteroids can be hundreds of miles wide. Others are only a few feet.

Most of our solar system's asteroids exist in the asteroid belt. This is a large cluster of asteroids between Mars and Jupiter. These asteroids are not packed tightly together. In fact, many are more than 1 million miles (1.6 million km) apart. Still, **collisions** happen.

When two asteroids collide, they often break into smaller asteroids. Sometimes, a small asteroid is captured by a larger asteroid's gravity. The small asteroid becomes the large asteroid's moon. Occasionally, two asteroids of the same size will orbit each other.

The asteroid belt contains more than 1 million asteroids.

Asteroids outside the asteroid belt are called Trojans. Trojans were captured by a planet's gravitational pull. They now orbit the planet. Jupiter has the most Trojans. But other Trojans orbit Mars, Neptune, and even Earth.

Scientists divide asteroids into three main **categories**. They are C-Type, S-Type, and M-Type. These categories are based on the asteroid's composition. Scientists learn what asteroids are made of by studying meteorites. They also study how much sunlight an asteroid reflects. The more metal an asteroid contains, the brighter it appears.

Most asteroids are C-Type. C-Type asteroids are made mostly of clay and **silicate** rocks. They reflect very little sunlight. S-Type asteroids are the second-most-common type. S-Type asteroids reflect some sunlight. They are made primarily of silicate rocks and **nickel-iron**.

M-Type asteroids are the rarest asteroids. They are also the brightest. M-Type asteroids are made almost entirely of nickel-iron.

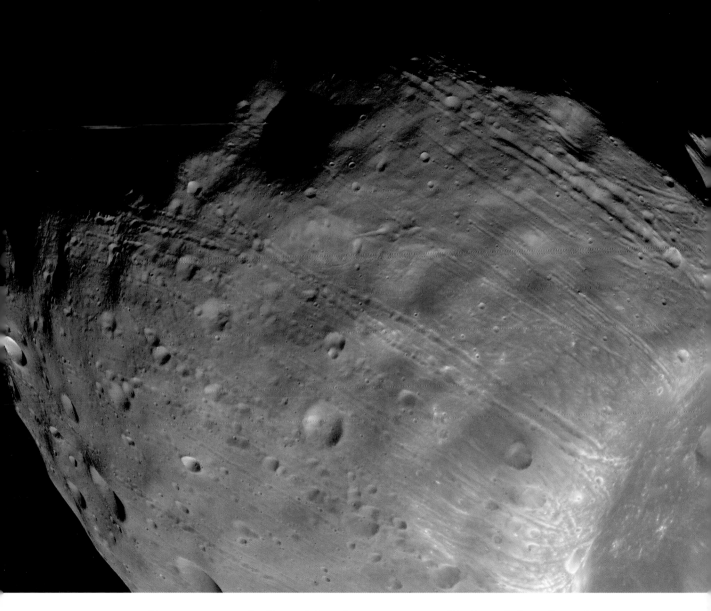

Astronomers believe Mars's two moons, Phobos (*above*) and Deimos, began as asteroids. They were captured by the planet's gravity.

CHAPTER 4

CONFUSING COMETS

Asteroids are often very small. They can rarely be seen from Earth without powerful telescopes. Because of this, they remained undiscovered until the 1800s. But humans have observed comets for much longer.

Ancient humans watched the night sky carefully. They used the regular movements of the stars to navigate and track seasons. In China, people recorded comet sightings as early as 1100 BCE. But comets puzzled these ancient stargazers. Unlike stars, they did not move in patterns. They seemed to show up with no warning.

DID YOU KNOW?

The word *comet* comes from the Greek word *komete*, which means "long-haired." Ancient Greeks called comets hairy stars because of their long tails.

In 1066, many people in England witnessed Halley's Comet. Soon after, English King Harold II was killed in battle. Some believed the comet was an omen of his defeat.

For more than 800 years, many saw comets as bad **omens**. Nobody knew what caused the bright streaks of light. But in the 300s BCE, Greek philosopher Aristotle took a guess. He believed comets were fires burning up in Earth's atmosphere. This idea was accepted for almost 2,000 years.

In 1577, Danish astronomer Tycho Brahe proved that comets exist outside of Earth's atmosphere. And in 1680, German astronomer Gottfried Kirch viewed a comet through a telescope. He was the first to do so. English mathematician Sir Isaac Newton calculated that comet's orbit. Astronomer Edmond Halley studied Newton's findings. He then calculated the orbits of other comets.

Meanwhile, telescopes grew more powerful. In 1801, Italian astronomer Giuseppe Piazzi discovered a new celestial object, Ceres. He believed Ceres was a planet. Astronomers discovered a similar object, Pallas, in 1802.

British astronomer William Herschel compared Ceres and Pallas to other planets and comets. Herschel decided the objects were something new. He named them asteroids.

DID YOU KNOW ?

Newton invented a new telescope to aid his celestial studies. It reflected light with mirrors instead of glass. Its simple design became very popular. We still use similar reflecting telescopes today.

SUPER SCIENTIST

EDMOND HALLEY

Edmond Halley was born in England on November 8, 1656. In the 1670s, he created a star location catalog. Later, using Newton's laws, Halley calculated the orbits of 24 comets. Surprisingly, three comets appeared to have the exact same orbits. They also appeared about once every 76 years. Halley believed these were actually the same comet. He predicted it would appear again in 1758.

Halley died in 1742. But his prediction was correct. The comet returned in 1758! It was later named Halley's Comet.

Halley's Comet at its most recent appearance in 1986

CHAPTER 5

STORY OF A METEOR

Throughout history, people thought meteorites were magical. Some cultures, including the Greeks, worshipped them. But they are simply stranded meteoroids.

Sometimes, Earth's gravity captures a nearby meteoroid. As the meteoroid passes through Earth's atmosphere, **friction** causes the object to heat up. Soon, the meteoroid's heat produces light. The streak of light is called a meteor, or shooting star.

Most meteoroids are tiny. They burn up completely. But sometimes, they are large enough to reach Earth. These meteoroids are called meteorites. Most are no bigger than a fist. But if a large meteorite hits Earth just right, its **impact** can leave an even larger crater.

Most meteorites look like partially melted rocks. But scientists classify them into three different groups.

This meteorite, nicknamed Black Beauty, was found in 2011. Scientists believe it may be the first meteorite to come from Mars.

They are based on the meteorite's composition. Stone meteorites are rocky. Iron meteorites are metallic. Stony-iron meteorites are a combination of the two.

CHAPTER 6

IMPACT!

Some meteoroids cause great destruction when they reach Earth. In 1902, a huge explosion occurred near Tunguska, Siberia. The explosion flattened trees for 800 square miles (2,000 sq. km). Scientists believe a massive meteor entered the atmosphere at 33,500 miles per hour (54,000 kmh). The meteor exploded just before reaching Earth. No crater or meteorite has been found.

Other meteors have been more destructive. About 65 million years ago, a six-mile-wide (10 km) meteor struck Earth. The **impact** left a crater more than 100 miles (161 km) wide. It also shot debris into the atmosphere, blocking all sunlight. This wiped out 75 percent of life on Earth.

Fortunately, such large impacts are rare. Scientists estimate they occur about once every 100 million years.

Most meteorites are found in Antarctica.
This is because they are easy to spot in the snow and ice.

Impacts of the size that occurred in Tunguska happen roughly once every 300 years. Still, scientists are constantly looking for near-Earth objects (NEOs) that could threaten our planet.

CHAPTER 7

HUNTING NEOS

Scientists still rely on telescopes to find and track asteroids. Today's telescopes can spot objects millions of **light-years** away. And some telescopes have special cameras. They photograph an area of sky over a period of time.

Scientists study these photographs carefully. They look for objects that change position between images. This indicates that the object is an asteroid or comet, rather than a **stationary** star. Infrared telescopes allow scientists to detect an asteroid or comet based on heat.

Scientists send spacecraft to study comets and asteroids up close. In 2004, the European Space Agency launched

DID YOU KNOW ?

Scientists have found evidence of water on both asteroids and comets.

24

NASA'S OSIRIS-REx spacecraft is tested at the Lockheed Martin Space Systems Facility. It will collect a soil sample from asteroid Bennu.

the spacecraft *Rosetta*. Its mission was to land on a comet. Along the way, *Rosetta* passed two asteroids. The spacecraft took measurements and photographs of the asteroids. *Rosetta* then sent the data back to scientists.

In 2007, the National Aeronautics and Space Administration (**NASA**) launched its *Dawn* spacecraft. From 2011 to 2016, *Dawn* visited the asteroids Vesta and Ceres. These are two of the largest asteroids in the asteroid belt. Scientists believe they have remained **intact** since the solar system began. Their composition could teach us about the beginning of our solar system.

Meanwhile, in November 2014, *Rosetta* landed on a comet. It was the first spacecraft to do so. *Rosetta* took many measurements and samples. It even found ice!

Upcoming missions could bring humans even closer to asteroids. In the 2020s, NASA plans to drag an asteroid into the moon's orbit. Astronauts could then explore the asteroid.

Scientists also continue to study as many NEOs as possible. A deadly **impact** from one of these objects is unlikely. But studying asteroids and comets is key to understanding Earth's past. And it will help protect our planet in the future.

TOOLS OF DISCOVERY

DEEP IMPACT

In 2005, NASA launched *Deep Impact*. The spacecraft was sent to crash into the comet Tempel 1. *Deep Impact*'s smaller component, the impactor, would separate from the main spacecraft, called the flyby.

On July 4, 2005, the impactor crashed into Tempel 1. The collision created a large crater. It also created a cloud of dust and debris. This cloud reached the flyby, which waited 300 miles (480 km) away. *Deep Impact* provided brand-new information about what a comet is made of.

The impactor was battery powered. It sent images to scientists up to the moment of its crash.

Famous Comets

Halley's Comet

- Identified in 1705 by Edmund Halley
- **Orbital Period**: 76 years
- First confirmed short-period comet

Shoemaker-Levy 9

- Discovered in 1993 by Eugene and Carolyn Shoemaker and David Levy
- Orbital period: No longer orbiting
- In July 1994, the comet crashed into Jupiter. This was the first **predicted collision** between two objects in our solar system.

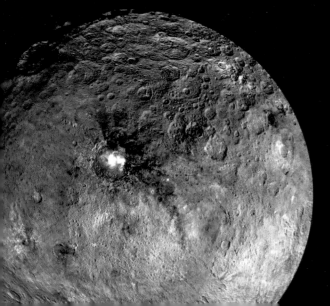

Ceres

Famous Asteroids

Ceres

- Discovered in 1801 by Giuseppe Piazzi
- Diameter: 584 miles (940 km)
- Largest asteroid in the asteroid belt. In 2006, scientists classified it as a dwarf planet.

Vesta

- Discovered in 1807 by Wilhelm Olbers
- Diameter: 327 miles (526 km)
- Brightest asteroid and the only asteroid visible without a telescope

Famous Meteoroids

Chicxulub

- Impact date: 65 million years ago
- The meteoroid wiped out 75 percent of life on Earth, including most of the dinosaurs.

Chelyabinsk Meteor Event

- Impact date: February 15, 2013
- A meteoroid broke up above Chelyabinsk, Russia. The event injured more than 1,500 people and damaged thousands of buildings.

GLOSSARY

category — a group of people or things that has certain characteristics in common.

collide — to come together with force. An act or instance of colliding is a collision.

core — the central part of a celestial body, usually having different physical properties from the surrounding parts.

friction — the force that resists motion between bodies in contact.

impact — the forceful striking of one thing against another.

intact — not broken or damaged.

light-year — the distance that light travels in one year.

NASA — National Aeronautics and Space Administration. NASA is a US government agency that manages the nation's space program and conducts flight research.

nickel-iron — a metal consisting of the elements nickel and iron.

omen — something that is believed to be a sign of a future event.

orbital period — the time taken for an object to make one complete orbit around another object.

predict — to guess something ahead of time on the basis of observation, experience, or reasoning.

silicate — a mineral that contains silicon and oxygen.

stationary — not moving or not able to be moved.

WEBSITES

To learn more about Exploring Our Universe, visit booklinks.abdopublishing.com. These links are routinely monitored and updated to provide the most current information available.

INDEX